The Jungle Book

Please visit our web site at: www.garethstevens.com
For a free color catalog describing Gareth Stevens Publishing's
list of high-quality books and multimedia programs,
call 1-800-542-2595 (USA) or 1-800-387-3178 (Canada).
Gareth Stevens Publishing's fax: (414) 332-3567.

Library of Congress Cataloging-in-Publication Data available upon request from publisher.
Fax (414) 332-2567 for the attention of the Publishing Records Department.

ISBN-13: 978-0-8368-7663-5 (lib. bdg.)

This North American edition first published in 2007 by
Gareth Stevens Publishing
A Member of the WRC Media Family of Companies
330 West Olive Street, Suite 100
Milwaukee, WI 53212 USA

This edition copyright © 2007 by Gareth Stevens, Inc. Original edition copyright © 2006
by La Galera SAU Editorial. World rights reserved. Original Spanish title: *El libro de la selva*.
Adaptation copyright © 2006 by Miguel Larrea. Illustrations copyright © 2006
by Javier Andrada

English translation: Belinda Bjerkvold
Gareth Stevens editor: Gini Holland
Gareth Stevens art direction: Tammy West
Gareth Stevens cover design: Scott M. Krall
Gareth Stevens production: Jessica Yanke and Robert Kraus

Printed in Canada

1 2 3 4 5 6 7 8 9 10 10 09 08 07 06

Illustrated Classics

The Jungle Book

Rudyard Kipling

GARETH**STEVENS**

GS

P U B L I S H I N G

A Member of the WRC Media Family of Companies

The moon lit the opening of a cave in the hills of Seeonee, India. Father Wolf left the cave, smelled the air, and stretched. Behind him came Mother Wolf. Four wolf cubs ran around her feet.

"It is a good night for hunting," said Father Wolf, pointing his nose to the sky.

He and Mother Wolf turned around quickly. A shadow was moving behind them! Tabaki, the jackal, crept into the clearing.

"I wish you luck and good hunting, Brother Wolf," said the jackal.

"We are not brothers, jackal," growled Mother Wolf. "If you sneak up on our den, you are looking for trouble."

"Calm down, Mother Wolf," said Tabaki. "I only came to tell you that Shere Khan is going hunting on these grounds."

"The tiger? That cowardly hunter?" asked Father Wolf. "May he be cursed! He will end up bringing us Man. He attacks Man's flock, so Man hunts him."

"The great tiger, Shere Khan, also has the right to eat," said Tabaki, and he let out a nasty laugh.

Mother Wolf raised the hairs on her spine.

"Get out of here, jackal," she said. "You have given us the news. Now go."

Frightening roars shattered the peace of the evening. The scared cubs howled and cried. "Is it the tiger?" they worried.

"There he is," said Father Wolf, "and it looks like he is following a trail."

"Shere Khan, the tiger that hates Man, is quick to make himself known," said Mother Wolf.

The bushes shook. Mother and Father Wolf crouched, ready to attack. A strange creature appeared before them. It was small and wobbly, without hair on its body. It stood up on its two back paws.

"I think it is a Man cub," whispered Father Wolf. He was not sure.

The creature let out a laugh when it saw them and wobbled up to play with the four cubs.

"Look at it," whispered Mother Wolf, fascinated. "It looks like a frog, but it has no fear of us."

"A Man cub can bring us many problems," Father Wolf whispered to Mother Wolf.

"That may be," said Mother Wolf, "but I like him. And right now, he is lost. Tonight, he will sleep with us."

The Man cub, a little boy, huddled among the wolf cubs in the back of the cave. Suddenly, the den got dark. The wolf family jumped up. A huge, striped head filled the opening of the cave.

"Good luck and good hunting," its voice growled.

"What are you looking for here, Shere Khan?" spit out Father Wolf.

"The Man cub," growled the tiger. "Bring him to me."

The wolves raised the hairs on their spines. Mother Wolf bared her teeth.

"Get out of here, striped cat, if you don't want to feel our teeth," she snarled.

Tabaki, the jackal, came up to the tiger. He whispered something in the tiger's ear. The two animals stood side by side.

"The cub is mine," growled the tiger. "I have been tracking him. Give him to me, and I will leave you in peace."

"Get out of here, hunter of babies," threatened Mother Wolf, "and take your stinking friend with you."

"I smell your Man cub, Shere Khan," said Tabaki. "He is there."

The eyes of the tiger blazed as his angry growl thundered over the walls of the cave.

"The Man cub belongs to me," roared the tiger, walking away. He saw the den was too small for fighting. "I have hunted him, and he will be mine."

Mother Wolf looked at the frightened boy and decided she would keep him. She called him *Mowgli*, or "Frog."

Mowgli's new family took him to the Council Rock. Here, all of the wolves of the Great Pack — and some other animals that were friendly with them — would decide if they would let Mowgli become a member of the pack.

While the wolves were talking about it, Shere Khan, the tiger, appeared at the foot of the Council Rock.

"Good hunting," he greeted them.

"The Council is meeting," said Akela, the leader of the pack. "You can't be here." Akela sat on the Council Rock and looked down on Shere Khan.

"I come only to get what is mine, Akela," growled the tiger. "What is a Man cub doing in your pack?"

"Quiet, tiger," snorted Akela. "You have no place in the Council. And all you wolves, look closely at the cub. Look at him, and vote."

The leader, Akela, and a few other wolves, said they should let the Man cub join. Some said no, because they feared Shere Khan. Baloo, the great brown bear, spoke in favor of Mowgli. Bagheera, the admired and feared black panther, offered the wolves a bull he had just killed. His gift would pay for Mowgli to come into the pack. Quickly, the hungry wolves said Mowgli could join the pack, and they took the bull to seal the agreement.

"The cub is mine," growled the tiger. "I was hunting him. You all are warned."

The boy Mowgli grew strong and healthy with the four wolf cubs. He learned to hunt with them. Thanks to his intelligence, he quickly became helpful to the pack when it hunted. He also helped when the pack fought with its enemies.

Father Wolf taught Mowgli the meanings of the sounds of the jungle. He also taught him the meanings of the scents carried by the wind. Bagheera, the black panther, became Mowgli's protector and most faithful friend. Bagheera taught Mowgli to climb the highest trees. After a little while, Mowgli was flying from branch to branch as fast as his new friends the monkeys.

Mowgli was happy in the jungle. He ate when he was hungry. He slept when he was tired. He went swimming in the lagoon with his best friends, Baloo and Bagheera, whenever he felt like it.

B aloo, the great brown bear, loved Mowgli as if the boy were his own cub. Baloo taught Mowgli the Laws of the Jungle. Baloo had been a teacher for many years, but he had never seen such a smart, good student. The first thing Baloo taught Mowgli was the magic words that were always used to greet strangers in the jungle: "Good hunting," which meant that strangers wished each other well.

Mowgli did not take long to learn the languages of the packs of the jungle. He could gossip about any animal with the porcupine, who seemed to know everything about everybody. Mowgli knew how to ask for favors from the snakes or the birds. He could give back the insults of Tabaki, the jackal, if he had to. Everyone in the jungle knew him and respected him. He was Mowgli, the Frog — and the Man.

For some time, the monkeys had watched the cheerful, smart Mowgli. They thought that if he were their king, the monkeys would be the most powerful pack in the jungle. If they could learn to throw a spear against an enemy the way Mowgli did — or if they knew how to make the clever traps that he made, or speak some of the languages that he spoke — the monkeys would have the rest of the animals at their feet.

Because of their hopes, the monkeys gave Mowgli wonderful fruits and nuts that only monkeys knew about. They gave him the most beautiful flowers. They turned flips in the branches of the trees and made funny faces to make him laugh.

Mowgli loved the way the monkeys treated him. One day, he went to Baloo the bear and Bagheera the panther and told them that the monkeys had asked him to be their king.

"Monkey Pack is the worst pack in the jungle!" yelled Baloo, blowing up. "They don't follow the Law."

"Don't let them take you," said Bagheera in his gentle voice. "They are cheaters and swindlers."

Mowgli looked at his friends for a few minutes in silence.

"A cheater is someone I hate more than anything," he said. "Of that I am sure. I promise, I will not go with them. I won't let them make me their king."

Mowgli always slept between Baloo and Bagheera. One dark night, he woke up suddenly. He felt furry paws. Many small, strong paws grabbed him by the arms and lifted him high off the ground. The branches and the leaves of the trees hit him in the face as he was pulled upward, and he heard the angry growls and roars of his friends below him. The monkeys were kidnapping Mowgli!

Bagheera tried to chase the kidnappers through the trees, but other monkeys threw sticks and rotten fruit while the first monkeys ran away with Mowgli. The panther and the bear ran after them on the ground, but the jungle kept them from going as fast as the monkeys, who were swinging through the treetops.

Mowgli closed his eyes as the monkeys jumped from branch to branch, high off the ground. With shrieks, pants, and snorts, they flew through the trees for hours, until they came to the huge ruins of a city covered by thick jungle. Mowgli had never been there.

Rann, the vulture, flying low, was the only one who saw where the monkeys took Mowgli.

19

In a few hours, Rann found Bagheera and Baloo. They were crying because they had lost Mowgli.

"Good hunting," greeted the vulture from a branch. "Have you perhaps lost our brother, Man cub?"

Bagheera and Baloo nodded.

"Talk, Rann," begged the panther. "What do you know of him?"

"The monkeys took him to the Hidden City," the vulture reported. "I saw him with my own eyes."

"But hundreds of monkeys live there. How will we rescue him?" asked Baloo.

"Only Kaa can help us," said Bagheera. "He is the only one that the monkeys fear."

Kaa, the python of 30 feet (9 meters), said he would help them save Mowgli. It took them all night to cross the jungle to the Hidden City. While the monkeys shrieked, played, and fought with each other, Mowgli sat, alone and sad, under some moss-covered stairs.

Kaa the snake, Bagheera, and Baloo attacked when the Sun set. Kaa hissed at the monkeys, tripped them, and pulled their tails as they ran away. Baloo hit the monkeys with his paws and bit them with his sharp teeth. Bagheera jumped on the monkeys with his sharp claws and snapped at them with his big jaws. Fighting the monkeys together, the three freed Mowgli by dawn. Crying with joy, Mowgli hugged his friends and licked their wounds.

Mowgli didn't want to know anything more about the monkeys. They were no longer his friends. Now he spent all his time with Baloo, Bagheera, and the wolves.

It was important to be liked in the jungle, but it was more important to be liked by the wolf pack. Akela, head of the pack, gave Mowgli the honor of leading the hunts. This honor made many of the young wolves jealous. They no longer liked Mowgli.

Shere Khan the tiger saw the jealousy that Mowgli caused, so he and Tabaki tried to feed that jealousy. If the wolf pack stopped protecting the boy, Shere Khan could hunt Mowgli and eat him.

"How can you all stand a Man cub leading you, the powerful Pack?" the tiger made fun of them.

"Are you all lap dogs?" added the jackal.

The wolves growled, puffing out fur on their necks.

"You should get rid of him at the next Council," suggested Shere Khan, "or within a short time, you will be his hunting dogs."

The wolves looked at each other with angry eyes.

The plans of Shere Khan and the wolves came to the ears of Bagheera and Baloo.

"They are jealous of you," said Bagheera to Mowgli. "Because of this, they hate you."

Mowgli's heart filled with sadness. The wolves had been plotting against him! Then, anger filled his chest.

"Those wolves that I always thought were my brothers now hate me," he said between his teeth, "but they are going to find out who I am. I will give them what they deserve."

Mowgli looked to the sky. "And to that cursed tiger, Shere Khan, I swear that — "

"No, Mowgli," Baloo stopped him. "If the wolves don't want you with them, the best you can do is to return to your own."

"My own? My own are the wolves," Mowgli replied sadly. "They are all of you."

"No, Mowgli," insisted Baloo. "You belong to the town of Man."

"But I —" sobbed Mowgli.

Bagheera the panther silently rubbed his smooth face against Mowgli's cheek.

"Now that they hate you, my master," he purred loudly, "give those traitors what scares them the most about Man. Scorch their snouts with the Red Flower."

"Fire?" Baloo exclaimed with fright.

The night of the Council meeting arrived. The family of wolves that had adopted Mowgli sat sadly among the many Council members who were against him.

"Not only has Mowgli helped us hunt better," said the pack leader, Akela, "over and over, he has used his hands to help us. Remember the many times he has taken the thorns out of your paws? Remember how often he set you free from the traps that you have fallen into?"

"But he is Man!" exclaimed Shere Khan, stepping out of the shadows. "Not one Man has ever ruled the pack."

"Be quiet, Shere Khan," growled Akela.

"You be quiet, Akela!" threatened the young wolves. "You are too old now. We want to know. Where is the little Man?"

Shere Khan the tiger smacked his lips, but in that moment, Mowgli jumped into the middle of the path where the wolves were meeting. He was holding a large, brightly burning torch.

"Here I am, jealous dogs," he yelled at them. "I'm going, but I will return to bring you the hide of this striped sack, Shere Khan. He will hunt me no more," Mowgli said, shaking the torch and frightening the wolves. "And you, jealous brothers, will hurt me no more."

Mowgli looked so angry that the wolves were afraid he would burn their fur.

Bagheera, Baloo, and Father Wolf walked Mowgli to the town of Man. They said goodbye to Mowgli at the edge of the jungle.

In a few months, Mowgli learned many of Man's words. The men in the town made him wear more clothing, and they cut his hair.

The town leader put Mowgli in charge of taking the buffalo to pasture. The town's buffalo fattened up nicely because Mowgli took them to the best pastures. These pastures were far away from the town. Here, Mowgli could be close to the jungle he still loved.

One day, while he was humming a song that he had learned in the town, Mowgli tripped over a rock in the shadows. Then he felt a snout rub his face. Mowgli pushed the snout away and jumped to his feet.

"Father Wolf!" yelled Mowgli, hugging him.

"You have lost your jungle ways," Father Wolf complained. "I could have bitten you with my fangs."

"You would never do that, dear Father," laughed Mowgli.

"Me, no," Father Wolf said, "but there is one who would do it happily."

Mowgli's face darkened.

"Shere Khan the tiger has left our hunting ground," said Father Wolf. "They have told me that he is coming through this way."

"He is coming here?" asked Mowgli.

"Yes," answered Father Wolf. "You already know why."

Mowgli took a deep breath. "That is fine," he growled like a wolf. "If he is looking for me, let him find me."

Mowgli decided it was time to rid the jungle of Shere Khan. With Father Wolf's help, he called a meeting with some of his jungle brothers, the wolf pack leader Akela, the panther Bagheera, and Baloo the bear. Other faithful wolves joined them, and Mowgli introduced them all to his buffalo herd.

"I have followed Shere Khan the tiger all evening." Father Wolf reported. "He has killed a deer and has eaten it to the bones. Now he is sleeping on the bank of the dry riverbed, beneath the cliff."

"If he has eaten, he will feel very heavy," observed Bagheera.

"That's it," said Mowgli. "This is the time. Listen to me well! The buffalo flock must be split into two . . . ."

Mowgli laid out the plan and gave each of them a job.

He sent the females of the buffalo herd with Akela to the bottom of the cliff, along the riverbed. The male buffaloes would charge from the top of the cliff, chased by Bagheera, Baloo, and the wolves. Riding the head buffalo, Mowgli would shout the signal to begin.

"Go!" Mowgli shouted. The male buffaloes rumbled down the cliff in a thick cloud of dust. The angry Shere Khan fled toward the lower part of the riverbed, but Akela drove the female buffaloes toward him. Hundreds of cattle trampled the tiger.

33

At the next Council meeting, the wolves argued. Some said that Mowgli had put an end to the tiger, but others were doubtful.

"How could Mowgli defeat the Striped One?" asked a young wolf. "A blow with his tiger paw would split the little man in half."

The wolves' growls and howls grew louder, then, suddenly, the wolves were quiet. Terror rose in their eyes as they saw a man walk toward them. He was holding a torch. It took them a moment to realize it was Mowgli. The wolves parted, growling fearfully as Mowgli made his path through the pack, waving the torch in front of him. In his other hand, Mowgli was carrying a sack.

"I trusted you all, my brothers," said Mowgli, "and I loved you."

The wolves lowered their heads, ashamed.

"You sent me away," he said, "but I have come to bring you that which I promised you." Mowgli reached his hand into the sack. Suddenly, he pulled out a huge, striped rug and threw it on the ground.

"Here is Shere Khan, who always tried to kill me," yelled Mowgli.

"It is the skin of Shere Khan," whispered the wolves. They did not dare lift their eyes.

"And, now, I leave you," Mowgli said. "You will not see me again."

Mowgli left the wolf pack without a backward look.

Mowgli had many others he wanted to say goodbye to. He had to thank the pack leader Akela, the two old gray wolves that were his parents, the younger wolves who were his brothers, a group of loyal wolves, and Baloo and Bagheera. Even Kaa the snake, whom most did not like, twisted around the branch of a tree to watch Mowgli leave.

Mowgli felt a knot in his stomach.

"You have been my family, and now, I have to leave you," he said sadly.

Bagheera brushed him with his velvety snout. "You will always be my friend," he purred.

"You are leaving us, dear Mowgli, but you will find your true family among Man," said Baloo, giving him a bear hug.

Mowgli stroked the necks of the wolves and hugged Mother Wolf and Father Wolf.

"I owe you my life," he told Mother and Father Wolf. "Thank you for taking care of me."

Everyone looked at Mowgli sadly. Then he turned and walked toward the town of Man. There, as Baloo said, he would find his true family. But that is another story.

About the Author

Born in India, Rudyard Kipling (1865–1936) was an English novelist and winner of the Nobel Prize in Literature, in 1907. He also received many honorary degrees and other awards, including the Gold Medal of the Royal Society of Literature, in 1926. Kipling is best known for his short stories, especially about India and Burma (now Myanmar), but he is also well known for his poetry. His *Jungle Book* was first published in 1904, and it quickly became a well-loved and internationally known children's classic.